Mama Rex & T

❦ Homework Trouble ❦

by Rachel Vail
Illustrations by Steve Björkman

ORCHARD BOOKS
An Imprint of Scholastic Inc.
New York

To my teachers Mrs. Sudak,
Mrs. T and Mrs. Barr, and Doc Murphy
—*RV*

For Carley Henderson, with love
—*SB*

Library of Congress Cataloging-in-Publication Data

Vail, Rachel.
Homework Trouble/by Rachel Vail; illustrations by Steve Björkman
p. cm. — (Mama Rex & T)
Summary: Mama Rex has plans for a fun afternoon with T until she learns that he has a diorama about pigs
due tomorrow, and so it's off to the library, the museum, and the park to gather information and supplies.

ISBN 0-439-40628-5—ISBN 0-439-42616-2 (pbk.)

[1. Dinosaurs—Fiction. 2. Homework—Fiction. 3. Mothers and sons—Fiction].
I. Björkman, Steve, ill. II. Title

PZ7.V1916 Ho 2002   [Fic]—dc21
2002017084
12 11 10 9 8 7 6 5 4 3 2 1   02 03 04 05 06

Book design by Elizabeth B. Parisi

Printed in Singapore 46
First trade printing, August 2002

Contents

Chapter 1
UH-OH

Mama Rex finished work early.

She went to T's school to pick him up.

She had the whole afternoon free.

Mama Rex waited on a bench for the door of T's classroom to open and thought about possibilities.

She and T could go to the library, or a museum, or the park.

Anywhere they wanted.

Mama Rex felt very happy.

Veronica's father sat down beside Mama Rex.

On his lap was a large wooden box with a forest scene inside.

There were tiny trees and bushes, and a family of deer nibbling at the leaves, beside a pond made from a mirror.

A laminated sign read DEER FORAGE IN THE FOREST.

"That's magnificent," said Mama Rex.

"It took all week," said Veronica's father. "What animal did T choose?"

"Excuse me?" said Mama Rex.

The classroom door swung open.
Children burst out.
T was surprised to see Mama Rex.
He ran over and gave Mama Rex a huge hug.
T loved being picked up by Mama Rex.

Mama Rex knelt down. "What animal did you choose?" asked Mama Rex.

"For my diorama?" asked T. "Pigs."

"Oh," said Mama Rex. "When do you have to bring in your diorama?"

"Tomorrow," said T.

"Oh," said Mama Rex.

T pulled a crumpled paper from his cubby. "I forgot to tell you."

"Oh, T," said Mama Rex. "I was planning a really fun afternoon with you. Going to the park or the museum or the library. Having some fun together."

T followed Mama Rex out of school.

"Don't worry," said T. "I can make a pig diorama in ten minutes, and then . . ."

Mama Rex zipped T's jacket. "Do you know anything about pigs?"

"Yes," said T. "I know one went to the market, and one stayed home. One ate roast beef . . ."

"Uh-oh," said Mama Rex.

T frowned. "Well, I know they love mud."

Mama Rex took T's hand and hurried across the street.

"Where are we going?" asked T.

"To the library," answered Mama Rex. "To learn about pigs."

"Hooray!" yelled T.

Chapter 2
HARD WORK

Mama Rex and T pushed through the turnstile, into the library.

"Hello," said Mama Rex to the woman behind the counter. "Are you a librarian?"

"I sure am," said the librarian.

"Great," Mama Rex said. "We're interested in pigs."

"Pigs are very interesting," said the librarian.

T smiled proudly. "I chose pigs for my diorama."

"And you need pig information," said the librarian.

T nodded.

The librarian walked out from behind the counter.
"You can start on the computer, right here."
Mama Rex and T sat down in front of the computer.
"Click here, then type in PIGS," said the librarian.
T pressed the keys.
The screen flipped around. Music played.
"There are 547 matches for pigs," read the librarian. "If the book you want isn't here, we can order it for you."
"It's due tomorrow," said Mama Rex.
"Oh," said the librarian. "Let's see what's here."

Mama Rex and the librarian clicked through the list.

T rested his head on the table.

He slid down to the floor and rested his head on his backpack.

There was a penny on the floor.

T crawled over and picked it up.

T rested his feet on a shelf and looked at the ceiling.

It was a boring ceiling.

T thought about ice cream.

"T!"

T looked over at Mama Rex and the librarian.

"Did you find something?" T asked.

"Did you?" asked Mama Rex.

"Yes," said T. "I found a penny." T showed her.

Mama Rex breathed through her nose.

T put the penny in his backpack and looked at the computer screen.

"Do you have that book?" T asked, pointing.

"Let's see," said the librarian.

The librarian led them to a maze of bookshelves.

T followed Mama Rex in. When Mama Rex stopped, T smashed into her.

He looked on the shelf beside them.

Pig books!

Mama Rex and T sat on the floor and opened books.

They learned that pigs are very smart, and that a pig's nose is called a snout.

T liked the word *snout*. "Snout, snout, snout," said T.

T chose two books to borrow, and carried them to the counter.

"Success!" whooped the librarian.

She waved a magic wand over the books. "Good luck with your diorama."

"Thanks," said T.

He followed Mama Rex into the cool afternoon.

"What *is* a diorama, anyway?"

"Uh-oh," said Mama Rex, grabbing T's hand and lifting her other.

A taxi screeched up beside them.

"Where are we going?" asked T, crawling in.

"To the Museum of Natural History," Mama Rex told T and the taxi driver, and slammed the door shut. "To see some dioramas."

"Hooray!" yelled T.

Mama Rex and T wandered through the towering halls of the Museum of Natural History, looking for the dioramas.

They each wore a maroon bracelet as a ticket.

T pretended his bracelet gave him superpowers. Mama Rex gave the map to T.

"Follow me," bellowed T superpowerfully.

They turned left, walked along, turned left again.

They found — the fire extinguisher.

"Hmm," said T, and looked at the map again. "This way!"

Mama Rex followed T.

They went up some stairs, around a corner, down a hall, into a dark alcove.

They found — the water fountain.

"Oh, good," said Mama Rex. "I was thirsty."

After Mama Rex and T drank some water, T studied the map again.

"Now I know," said T.

Mama Rex followed T around to the left and found — some folded chairs.

They went down a hall and discovered — the gift shop.

They turned right twice, and found — the café.

"I wish I were smart," said T. "Like a pig."

"You're smart like a dinosaur," said Mama Rex.

T spun around and found —

"A diorama!" yelled Mama Rex. "Magnificent."

Mama Rex and T stared through the glass at the family of bears, sitting in a field with a few trees and bushes, some grass, and behind them a painting of the forest.

"I have to make something like *that*?" T whispered.

"Smaller," said Mama Rex.

"And with pigs," said T.

Mama Rex and T wandered around looking at
the magnificent dioramas.

They sat on a bench. T rested his heavy head
on Mama Rex's lap.

"Maybe I'll have a sore throat tomorrow,"
suggested T.

Mama Rex stood up.

T tumbled off the bench onto the floor.

"Come on," said Mama Rex. "We need stuff to
make a pig habitat."

T followed Mama Rex out the heavy museum
doors and down the stone steps.

"Where can we get it?" asked T.

Mama Rex took T's hand. They waited for the light to change.

"The park?" asked T.

Mama Rex nodded.

"Hooray!" whispered T, dragging his tired feet across the street.

Chapter 3
WALLOWING

Mama Rex and T straggled into their apartment.

T dumped his backpack onto some newspaper.

He had twigs, leaves, acorns, dirt, the crusts left over from his lunch, two library books, and a penny.

"We need a box," mumbled T.

"Uh-oh," said Mama Rex.

Into T's closet went Mama Rex.

Out flew a pair of snow pants, fourteen balls, seven checkers, a sleeping bag, and half of Pinocchio.

"Pflut!" yelled Mama Rex.

T dug through his stuffed animal collection and discovered — Mama Rex.

"I have an idea," said Mama Rex, holding up her hand.

T yanked her up.

"I'll be right back," Mama Rex said. "Start making pigs."

T took out his art box.

He drew a picture of a pig and cut it out.

Mama Rex came back with a cup of coffee for herself, a cup of water for T, and an empty cottage cheese tub.

"It's all we've got," she said.

T stood his pig in the cottage cheese tub.

The pig fell down.

T glued a stick to the back of the pig.

The pig fell down again.

T stacked pom-poms behind the pig.

The pig fell down.

T fell down, too.

"I hate dioramas!" yelled T.

"Maybe you could draw a pigpen," suggested Mama Rex. "And glue the pig to it, in the bottom of the tub."

"It's supposed to stand up," yelled T. "In the museum all the dioramas were stand-uppy!"

"True," said Mama Rex.

"Mine is going to look like 'how a pig sleeps!'" groaned T. "No time. No ideas. No box. And a lazy pig that looks like a surprised pink school bus. I can't do it!"

"Maybe we should read a bit more," suggested Mama Rex, and opened one of the library books. "Maybe that'll give you some ideas."

T flopped onto the floor, which toppled his cup into his dirt pile.

"Ugh!" yelled T, grabbing his cup.

"Mud," said Mama Rex.

T sat up.

He took the book from Mama Rex and found a page with muddy pigs on it.

"My diorama could be made of mud," whispered T, pointing at the mud spreading toward his pig on the newspaper.

"Wait a sec," said Mama Rex, and read, "'Pigs
like to keep clean and cool. When it gets hot,
pigs roll around in water to cool off. They wallow
in mud only if there's no water.'"

"They don't even love mud?" groaned T.

"Unless mud is all they can find," said Mama Rex.

T smiled. "Mud is all MY pig can find."

T filled the plastic tub with dirt.

He added the rest of his water and stirred with a stick.

When it was gloppy, T nudged his pig's legs deep into the mud.

On a piece of paper T wrote, A PIG WALLOWS IN MUD WHEN ALL HE'S GOT IS MUD.

T glued the strip of paper to the outside of the cottage cheese tub.

A pig wallows in mud when all he's got is mud.

T held up his diorama for Mama Rex to see.

"What do you think of it?" T asked Mama Rex.

"It's yours," said Mama Rex. "What do you think of it?"

"Well," T said. He looked at his diorama from every angle. "I guess it's between OK and good."

"I think more toward good," said Mama Rex.

"Maybe," said T proudly. "But our afternoon together was magnificent."

"Yes," said Mama Rex. "They always are."